Uggy and Pal:

The 'Best Friend Forever' problem

By Jamie O'Dowd
Illustrated by Kirsty McKay

A 'Read, Talk and Play' book

Uggy and Pal:

How to use this 'Read, Talk and Play' Book

This story is divided into three sections. At the end of each section there are some 'talk it through' questions to discuss about the situation the characters find themselves in and how they might go about resolving them. There are also some 'play it out' scenarios where drama can be used to explore how the behavior of the characters affects those around them. The young readers can take on the role of one of the main characters and show how they might respond if they were in a similar situation.

Uggy's story

Uggy and Pal were in class 1B and were best friends forever.

But Pal didn't want to play with Uggy anymore.

Uggy felt sad. Pal was supposed to be his best friend forever.

It was playtime at school. Uggy usually played tag or football with Pal but today Pal was playing with some other children from a different class.

In the busy and noisy playground Uggy felt all alone.

Pal used to be his best friend forever.

Mrs Fearn saw that Uggy was all by himself. 'What's the matter Uggy? Why aren't you playing chase or football with Pal?' she said with a sunny smile.

She put her arm around Uggy.

'No one wants to play with me,' he said.

Mrs Fearn sat down on the wall next to Uggy. Together they watched the children as they ran around having fun. Some children started a game of football while the younger children played in the sand pit under the shade of an oak tree.

'Now then, Uggy, why doesn't anyone want
to play with you?' she asked.

'It's not my fault!' he began, 'These boys and girls are mean!' Uggy pointed at the children in the playground. 'When we play tag, they tell the teacher on me – just because I'm super-fast and always win!'

'My, my. That's not very kind,' Mrs Fearn said with a shake of her head. 'Tell me more, Uggy.'

'And, when we're playing football, no one ever picks me for their team just because I am the best,' Uggy said, his mouth turned down like an upside-down banana.

'What a shame,' cried Mrs Fearn 'I know how much you love football.'

A big cheer went up from the field as a goal flew into the back of the net.

Uggy wiped a tear from his eye. Some children from his class ran past, laughing and shouting each other's names.

'There, there, Uggy. Don't be upset. Tell me everything and we'll sort this out for you,' Mrs Fearn said. She had a kind face, a little bit like a smiling sun.

'When we play in the sand together, everyone runs off and hides from me,' Uggy said. He put his head in his hands.

'Oh dear, we can't have that.' Mrs Fearn shook her head. 'I think we should speak to Pal and try and get this fixed. What do you think to that, Uggy?' she asked.

'Erm, well okay then, Mrs Fearn.' he said, wiping his eyes with the sleeve of his school jumper.

Talk it through...

1. Why do you think Uggy is feeling sad?

2. Why might Pal have decided not to play with Uggy anymore?

3. What could Uggy do to try and make things better?

4. What do you think the teacher will do to try and make things better?

5. What would you do if your best friend didn't want to play with you anymore?

Play it out...

1. Play out what you think will happen next to Uggy and Pal.

2. What will Mrs Fearn say to Pal?

3. What might Pal have to say to Uggy?

Pal's story

The bell rang for the end of playtime. The children streamed into their lines and waited for their teachers to lead them back into class. Uggy was still sat on the wall. He felt a bit embarrassed. Mrs Fearn called out, 'Pal, can I have a little word with you please?'

13

Pal left the line and sat on the wall next to Mrs Fearn.

His cheeks were red from running around and he was still a little out of breath. 'Uggy says you don't want to play with him anymore, is that true? I thought you two were best friends forever?'

'We *were* been best friends forever,' said Pal. He looked at Uggy, 'But when we play tag, Uggy trips people over or pulls us around by our shirts.'

Pal rolled up his school trousers and showed Mrs Fearn the red scabs on his knees 'See?' he said.

Uggy looked down at the ground.

'And what's this about leaving him out when you play football?' asked Mrs Fearn.

'Well, I don't like playing football with Uggy anymore,' Pal said. 'When he scores a goal he pulls faces at me and calls me "monkey face!"'

Pal showed his teacher the monkey face
by sticking out his tongue, pulling out his
ears and grunting.

Uggy squirmed as he listened. 'Well, that's not very kind,' Mrs Fearn said. 'So, what about when you play in the sand? Why do you run away from Uggy? That doesn't sound very nice!'

Uggy put his fingers in his ears. He didn't want to hear Pal's answer.

'Because Uggy calls himself the "Stinky Sand Monster". He picks up the sand and spins around spraying it in everyone's face! We have to run away from him because it really hurts to get sand in your eyes!'

'I'm sure it does, Pal.' Mrs Fearn turned to Uggy. 'Is this true Uggy? Have you been doing all these things that Pal has told me?'

Uggy was still looking at the ground. 'I was just having fun,' he mumbled. 'I thought Pal would find it funny.'

'Uggy, I think we need to have a little talk about what it means to be a best friend forever....'

Talk it through...

1. Why doesn't Pal want to play with Uggy anymore?

2. What do you think Mrs Fearn should say to him?

3. What could he do to try and be a better friend to Pal?

4. Has Pal done the right thing by not playing with Uggy?

5. What would you do if someone wasn't playing nicely in the playground?

Play it out...

1. Play out what you think Mrs Fearn might say or do to Uggy now she knows the truth about what has been happening?

2. How might Uggy and Pal solve their best friend forever problem?

How to solve a best friend problem

Mrs Fearn taught the boys a special way to make sure they never have a best friend problem again. It was a little rhyme. She told them to say it whenever they were unsure if what they were doing was kind. It goes like this:

"Is this gentle? Is this nice?
If it isn't, please think twice."

It made Uggy very sad to think that he had made Pal feel unhappy by playing rough. Pal really was his best friend forever and it didn't feel good being all by himself at playtime. Uggy said sorry to Pal and they shook hands with their special secret club handshake that only they knew about.

The next time they played tag together Uggy thought about tripping Pal over to try and win. Then he stopped and remembered the rhyme. He said it to himself in his head. Instead of sticking out his foot to trip him, he decided to slow down to let Pal catch him so everyone had a chance to win.

Pal saw this and said to Uggy, 'Best friends forever.'

The next time they played football Uggy scored a fantastic goal. When he thought about pulling the monkey face, he stopped and remembered Mrs Fearn's rhyme.

Instead of being mean, Uggy gave Pal a high five, 'Good goal, Uggy,' said Pal. 'Best friends forever.'

In the sandpit Uggy chose not to be the 'Stinky Sand Monster'. Instead, when some younger children from the nursery started throwing sand around and some nearly went into Pal's eye, he remembered the best friend rhyme. In his nicest voice, Uggy asked them to 'Please stop.'

Pal thanked him, 'Best friends forever' he said.

ouch!

28

From under the shade of the oak tree, Mrs Fearn watched the two boys playing together. She loved to see the smiles on their faces again. She really believed they would go on to be best friends forever.

Talk it through...

1. What did Uggy do to become Pal's best friend again?

2. How does Uggy feel now, compared to at the start of the story?

3. How does Pal feel now compared to at the start of the story?

4. Why is it important to play nicely with other people?

5. Uggy and Pal decide to make 3 rules about being best friends – what sort of best friend rules might they make to ensure they never fall out?

Play it out...

1. Play out some examples of Uggy and Pal playing nicely.

2. Act out what it means to be best friends forever.

11374010R00020

Printed in Great Britain
by Amazon.co.uk, Ltd.,
Marston Gate.